This book is created for every single child: girls, boys, and kids who identify as both or neither. Be exactly who you are!

—LG and JH

For Erzsi. Thank you for always believing in me and my writing. Thank you for being my partner in bringing stories with humor, heart, and hope into the world.

—LG

A PROUD PARTNERSHIP BETWEEN

glaad + b BONNIER Publishing USA

A portion of the proceeds from the sale of this book will be donated to accelerating LGBTQ acceptance.

This is for my parents and brother, for always playing along, whether it was with fire trucks, tea sets, or mermaid dolls. Imagination and love always came first. Thank you!

—JH

little bee books
an imprint of Bonnier Publishing USA

251 Park Avenue South, New York, NY 10010 | Text copyright © 2019 by Laura Gehl | Illustrations copyright © 2019 by Joshua Heinsz
Book design by David DeWitt | All rights reserved, including the right of reproduction in whole or in part in any form. | Little Bee Books is a trademark of Bonnier Publishing USA, and associated colophon is a trademark of Bonnier Publishing USA. | Manufactured in China TPL 0419 | First Edition
1 3 5 7 9 10 8 6 4 2

Library of Congress Cataloging-in-Publication Data
Names: Gehl, Laura, author. | Heinsz, Joshua, illustrator. | Title: Except when they don't / by Laura Gehl; illustrated by Joshua Heinsz. | Other titles: Except when they do not | Description: First edition. | New York, NY: Little Bee Books, 2019. | Summary: Illustrations and simple, rhyming text challenge the idea that boys and girls should each wear only certain colors or play with certain toys, and encourages them to be true to themselves.
Identifiers: LCCN 2018047220 | Subjects: | CYAC: Stories in rhyme. | Gender role—Fiction. | Individuality—Fiction. | Play—Fiction. | BISAC: JUVENILE FICTION / Family / General (see also headings under Social Issues). | JUVENILE FICTION / Imagination & Play. | JUVENILE FICTION / Toys, Dolls, Puppets.
Classification: LCC PZ8.3.G273 Exc 2019 | DDC [E]—dc23 | LC record available at https://lccn.loc.gov/2018047220

ISBN 978-1-4998-0804-9 | littlebeebooks.com | bonnierpublishingusa.com

EXCEPT WHEN THEY DON'T

WORDS BY
LAURA GEHL

PICTURES BY
JOSHUA HEINSZ

little bee books

Boys play monster trucks with glee.

Girls bake cakes and serve hot tea.

Girls like pom-poms,
pink, and jewels.

Boys like fighting
pirate duels.

Girls sashay in sparkly shoes.
Boys wear clothes of only blue.

Boys cut bad guys down to size.
Girls paint purple butterflies.

Except when they don't.

Boys build spaceships
out of blocks.

Girls delight
in princess frocks.

Girls think ponies are a blast.

Boys like race cars, loud and fast.

Girls perform to fairy songs.

Boys play football all day long.

Boys yell, "Boo!" and run away.

Girls like kittens and ballet.

Except when they don't.

You might play with swords and knights.
Maybe twirl in flowered tights.

You might tuck bears into bed.

Or put earthworms on your head.

You might like to paint your nails.
Maybe hike on nature trails.

You might make a lot of noise.
Or take baths with mermaid toys.

You might think you need to choose
dolls or robots, pinks or blues. . . .

Except that you don't.

Girls and boys like lots of things:
Play-Doh, puzzles, queens and kings,
dressing up and making forts,
playing house and playing sports.

Flying planes and driving cars,

hanging from the monkey bars,

gazing up at distant stars,

rock 'n' rolling with guitars.

Everywhere from near to far . . .

. . . be exactly who you are!